TAP THE MAGIC TREE

TAP THE MAGIC TREE

Christie Matheson

GREENWILLOW BOOKS
An Imprint of HarperCollinsPublishers

There's magic in this bare brown tree.
Tap it once.
Turn the page to see.

Tap again—

one,
two,
three,
four.

Now tap again, even more!

Rub the tree to make it warm.

Touch each bud

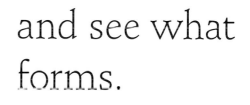

and see what forms.

Give the tree a little jiggle.

That's it.

Now make your
fingers wiggle.

Brush away the petals (swish!)
and blow the tree a tiny kiss.

Shake the tree. . . .

Plop!

Plop!

Plop!

Plop!

Plop!

Plop!

Kerplop!

Knock, knock on the trunk,

then stop.

Pat the leaves—be gentle, please.

Aha!
Now blow a whooshing breeze.

Clap your hands to bring . . .

the snow!

Okay.
Be patient. . . .

Wait! Don't go!

Close your eyes and count to ten.

Magic!
It begins again.

for Ellie and Jack

Tap the Magic Tree
Copyright © 2013 by Christie Matheson.
For information address HarperCollins Children's Books,
a division of HarperCollins Publishers,
10 East 53rd Street, New York, NY 10022.
www.harpercollinschildrens.com

Collages were used to prepare the full-color art.
The text type is 30-point Stempel Schneidler.

Library of Congress Cataloging-in-Publication Data

Matheson, Christie, author, illustrator.
Tap the magic tree / by Christie Matheson.
pages cm
"Greenwillow Books."
Summary: Invites the reader to tap, rub, touch, and wiggle
illustrations to make an apple tree bloom, produce fruit, and lose its leaves.
ISBN 978-0-06-227445-8 (trade ed.)
[1. Stories in rhyme. 2. Apples—Fiction. 3. Trees—Fiction. 4. Seasons—Fiction.] I. Title.
PZ8.3.M4227Mak 2013 [E]—dc23 2013001035

First Edition
13 14 15 16 17 SCP 10 9 8 7 6 5 4 3 2 1

 Greenwillow Books